Wolf Story

WOLF STORY

by William McCleery

WITH ILLUSTRATIONS BY

WARREN CHAPPELL

LINNET · BOOKS

1988

© 1947 William McCleery. All rights reserved.
Published 1988 as a Linnet Book,
an imprint of The Shoe String Press, Inc.,
North Haven, Connecticut 06473. First published 1947 as
a Borzoi Book, an imprint of Alfred A. Knopf, Inc.

Library of Congress Cataloging-in-Publication Data

McCleery, William.
   Wolf story.
   Summary: A young father tells his five-year-old son humorous
variations on the theme of a hen escaping the clutches of a wily wolf.
   [1. Wolves—Fiction. 2. Fathers and sons—Fiction. 3. Story-
telling—Fiction. 4. Humorous stories] I. Chappell, Warren,
1904-   ill. II. Title
PZ7.M478413Wo   1988   [Fic]   87-25977
ISBN 0-208-02191-4 (alk. paper)

The paper used in this publication meets the minimum requirements
of American National Standard for Information Sciences—
Permanence of Paper for Printed Library Materials,
ANSI Z39.48-1984. ∞

Manufactured in the United States of America

For Mike

Wolf Story

Chapter 1

NCE upon a time a man was putting his five-year-old son Michael to bed and the boy asked for a story.

"All right," said the man.

"Well, let me see. Oh yes. Well, once upon a time there was a girl with long golden hair and they called her Goldilocks."

"No, no," said the boy. "A *new* story."

"A new story?" said the man. "What about?"

"About a hen," said the boy.

"Good!" said the man. "I was afraid you might want another wolf story. Well, once upon a time there was a hen." The man stopped.

"Go on," said the boy. "What are you waiting for?"

"What is a good name for a hen?"

Michael looked very thoughtful. "Make it that the hen's name is . . . Rainbow," he said.

"Why Rainbow?" asked the father.

"Because," said the boy, "he had all different colored feathers."

"He?" said the man.

"She," said the boy.

"All right," said the man. "But you understand that there is no such thing as a hen with all different colored feathers." The man did not like to tell his son things that were not true.

"I know, I know," said the boy. "Go on."

And the man continued. "Once upon a time there was a hen. She was called Rainbow because her feathers were of many different colors: red and pink and purple and lavender and magenta—" The boy yawned. —"and violet and yellow and orange . . ."

"That will be enough colors," said the boy.

"And green and dark green and light green . . ."

"Daddy! Stop!" cried the boy. "Stop saying so many colors. You're putting me to sleep!"

"Why not?" said the man. "This is bedtime."

"But I want some story first!" said the boy. "Not just colors."

"All right, all right," said the man. "Well, Rainbow lived with many other hens in a house on a farm at the edge of a deep dark forest and in the deep dark forest lived a guess what."

"A wolf," said the boy, sitting up in bed.

"No, sir!" cried the man.

"Make it that a wolf lived in the deep dark forest," said the boy.

"Please," said the man. "Anything but a wolf. A weasel, a ferret, a lion, an elephant . . ."

"A wolf," said the boy.

"Well, all right," groaned the man, "but please don't sit up in bed. Put your head on your pillow and shut your eyes."

"O.K.," said the boy. He turned his pillow over so that it would be cool against his cheek.

"So," said the man. "In the forest lived a stupid old wolf, too tired to do any harm."

"No!" cried the boy, sitting up in bed again. "The wolf is *fierce!* Terribly terribly fierce!!"

"Haven't we had enough stories about terribly fierce wolves?" cried the man.

"No!"

"All right," said the man. "A terribly terribly fierce wolf with red eyes and teeth as long and sharp as butcher knives."

"Mmmmmmm," said the boy, putting his cheek on his pillow again and shutting his eyes.

"I suppose you like that about the butcher knives," said the man.

"I love it," said the boy. "Go on."

"Well, one night when it was very dark the wolf came slinking out of the forest. By the way, what is the wolf's name?"

"Waldo," said the boy.

"No, no," said the man.

"Yes, yes," said the boy.

"But Waldo was in our last story! He's been in every story since Christmas. Can't we ever have a new one?"

The boy shook his head. "No, because Waldo is the fiercest wolf in all the world!"

"Put your head on the pillow," said the man.

The boy put his head on the pillow. "Go on," he said.

"Well, this wolf named Waldo came slinking out of the forest very quietly," whispered the man. "Very *very* quietly. In fact nobody could hear him."

"Talk a little louder," said the boy. "I can't hear *you.*"

"Michael," said the man. "If you open your mouth once more I will stop telling the story and go downstairs."

"All right," said the boy. "But what did the wolf do when he slinked out of the forest?"

"Slunk," said the man.

"Slunk," said the boy.

"Or maybe *slank,*" said the man.

"Make it that he crawled out of the forest," said the boy, "but go on!!"

"Michael!" said the man. "You were not to open your mouth!"

"I was helping," said the boy.

"Don't do it again. Well, so the wolf Waldo crawled out of the forest one night when the moon was bright and crept over to the hen house. For a long time the wolf had been watching Rainbow with his big red eyes. He wanted to eat the hen and save her pretty feathers to make an Indian headdress." The boy smiled because he knew it was a joke. A wolf would never think of making an Indian headdress. He would have laughed but he was too sleepy. "The feathers were so beautiful," said the man. "Red and pink and purple and lavender."

"Oooohhh!" yawned the boy.

"And magenta . . . and . . . violet . . . and . . . yellow . . ."

The man got up quietly from where he had been sitting on the bed beside the boy. He opened the window and pulled the blanket up around the boy's chin and crept quietly out of the room, almost as quietly as the wolf Waldo. The boy was sound asleep.

Chapter 2

THE next evening the boy went upstairs and got ready for bed all by himself. He took off his clothes and left them on the floor, accidentally kicking one shoe under the bed where it would be hard to find the next morning. He also accidentally dropped his underpants in the wastebasket. Then he pulled on his blue flannel pajamas, the ones with long flannel feet, and went to the head of the stairs. He called to his father who had promised to put him to bed again.

His father came upstairs.

"Did you brush your teeth?" he said.

"When?" said the boy.

"Tonight."

"Not tonight, no," said the boy. "Shall I?"

"Why not?" said the man. "And what about washing your face?"

"All right."

"Shall I help you?"

"No, no, no," said the boy, quickly. If there was anything he hated worse than washing his face it was having someone else wash it.

"I'll be straightening your room," said the man.

The boy hurried to the bathroom and climbed up on the little white steps below the wash basin. He smeared toothpaste first on his toothbrush and then on his teeth. He took a big mouthful of water, swushed it around and spit it out. That was supposed to be brushing his teeth. Then he took a damp washcloth and gently touched his face with it, being careful not to disturb the dirt inside his ears. He threw the washcloth down, dried his hands on his flannel pajamas, raced into the bedroom and leapt onto the bed. His father looked at him.

"Some day you'll wear out your face, washing it so hard," he said. The boy laughed and jerked the covers down from the top. Then he crawled under the covers clear to the bottom of the bed and curled up there like a grub worm.

"Come out of there," said the man. "I haven't got all night." The boy didn't move. "Come on. Please. Hurry up," said the man. The boy did not move. The man reached under the covers and tickled the boy, and pulled him up to the top of the bed.

"Tell about Rainbow," said the boy.

"Who?" said the man. "Rainbow? Oh yes. Well, if I'm going to tell about Rainbow I won't have time for songs."

The boy did not feel like making a fuss. "Just tell about Rainbow," he said. "But make it long."

So the man continued the story where he had left off the night before.

"The wolf Waldo crept very quietly to the chicken yard. He was quiet because he did not want to wake up Mr. Tractor-wheel."

The boy asked in a loud voice, "Mr. *WHO?*"

"Tractorwheel. Isn't that a good name for a farmer?"

"Very good, Daddy," said the boy. "And make it that Mr. Tractorwheel has a son."

"He has several sons. And the wolf didn't want to wake up any of them."

"He didn't want to wake up the hens, either," said the boy.

"Because the hens would make so much noise *they* would wake up Mr. Tractorwheel and his sons," said the man.

"Yes," said the boy, "and Mr. Tractorwheel would come running with a shotgun and shoot the wolf."

"Don't you want the wolf to be shot?" said the man.

"Yes," said the boy, "but not yet. It has to be a long story first."

"I see," said the man. "Well, when the wolf came to the chicken yard, what did he find?"

"Rainbow!" cried the boy.

"No," said the man. "Rainbow is in the hen house asleep. But what is all around the chicken yard?"

The boy sat up in bed, thinking hard. Then he said, "A fence."

The man was surprised.

"A fence is right!" he said. "You're a smart boy." The boy smiled and lay down again, this time on his back, with his hands clasped under his head and his elbows sticking out on either side like wings.

"The chicken yard was entirely surrounded by a fence," said the man, "and the gate was locked. So how could Waldo the wolf get inside to capture Rainbow?"

"Make it that there is a hole in the fence," said the boy.

"No," said the man. "If there was a hole in the fence, the chickens would get out and wander into the forest, and the wolf would be so busy catching and eating them he wouldn't have time to come after Rainbow."

"Could he climb over the fence?" said the boy.

"You know a wolf couldn't climb a fence," said the man.

"But this is only a story," said the boy. "You can make anything happen in a story."

"He might go under the fence," said the man.

"Ooooohhh!" the boy yawned. "Hurry up and get him in somehow."

"Well, the wolf began to dig with his

sharp toe-nails in the soft earth until he had dug a tunnel right under the fence. Then he crawled through the tunnel and came out in the chicken yard. Very quietly he crept over to the hen house. Very quietly. In fact very

. . . v-e-r-y . . . v——e———r———y . . . quietly." The boy yawned again and turned over on his side.

The man waited for a moment and then stood up, thinking the boy was asleep. But without opening his eyes the boy flung out one hand and caught his father's arm.

"Go on," he said. "More."

The man sat down again.

"In the hen house he looked around until he saw a hen with all different colored feathers. Blue and gray and scarlet and . . . vermilion . . . and . . . cobalt . . . and . . . azure."

Now the boy was really asleep and the man turned out the light, opened the window, pulled up the covers and kissed the boy on the cheek. On his way out of the darkened room he stumbled over the tin wastebasket and made a terrible clatter, but the boy was too deep in sleep to be bothered by anything at all.

Chapter 3

HE next day was Sunday and at breakfast the man said to the boy, "Shall we go on an excursion today?"

"Yes!" cried the boy.

"To Central Park," said the man.

"Fort Tryon Park!" cried the boy.

"But that is so *far away!*" said the man.

"And let's take Steffy," said the boy.

Steffy's real name was Stefan and he lived next door. He was a year older than Michael.

"All right," said the man. "We could have lunch up there. Do you mind if we have lunch in the park?" said the boy's father to the boy's mother. "Would you mind not having to fix lunch for us?"

"Oh, that would be terrible," said the boy's mother. "If I don't have to fix lunch for you I will be forced to go back to bed and read the Sunday papers!"

Soon the man and the two boys were driving along the West Side Highway toward Fort Tryon Park. The boys could see freighters, tankers, ferryboats and other craft in the Hudson River. "Enemy battleships!" the boys cried, and raked them with fire from their wooden rifles. Sometimes the man had to speak sternly to the boys, saying, "Boys! Sit down! Stop waving those rifles around. Do you want to knock my front teeth out?"

The boys were very well behaved, and every time the man spoke sternly to them they would stop waving the rifles around, for a few seconds anyway.

When they came to Fort Tryon Park they parked the car near the entrance.

"Let's see if our treasure is still there!" said Michael.

"Let's see if my front teeth are still there," said his father.

"What treasure?" said Stefan.

"Come on," said Michael. "I'll show you."

They walked down some stone steps and along a walk until they came to a broken-down fence. Beyond the fence was a very steep hill, so steep that the trees had to hold on by their bare roots to keep from slipping. In a hole at the base of one of those trees, Michael and his father had hidden a rusty old paper-punch several weeks before. They scrambled down the hill until they found the tree, and sure enough, the paper-punch was still there; a little rustier, perhaps—in fact ready to fall apart—but still there. They put it back in the same hiding place and then worked their way carefully down the hill, through a high arched tunnel and up to a big green playfield where the boys chased each other until lunch time.

After lunch in the park restaurant they sat on a bench eating Cracker Jack. Michael was disappointed because the prize in his Cracker Jack box was just a piece of cardboard with numbers on it; a silly game of some kind; and Steffy's prize was a beautiful bright green cardboard monkey. Michael asked for another box of Cracker Jack, hoping that next time he might get a prize like Steffy's, but his father said no.

"The prize you get in a Cracker Jack box is a matter of luck," said Michael's father.

"What's luck?" said Michael.

"Something that happens and you have to be satisfied with."

There were tears in Michael's eyes.

"Damn it," he said.

"You mean *darn* it," said his father.

"Is *damn* a bad word?" said Michael, rather eagerly.

"No-o-o," said his father, "but it is more a word for grownups. A boy your age could say *darn* it."

"Darn it," said Michael. "Darn it, darn, darn, darn. Steffy, would you give me your monkey? I'll be your *best friend!*"

Stefan shook his head. "You're already my best friend," he said.

Michael walked sadly away from the bench toward a big wire wastebasket at the edge of the walk. He looked into the wastebasket. Suddenly he shouted..

"Daddy! Come here quick, Daddy!"

There in the wastebasket was a beautiful bright green cardboard monkey exactly like Stefan's. Someone had thrown it away. It was not dirty. Not folded, even. The man took it out of the basket and gave it to his son, and now both boys were happy.

"What about taking a rest," said the man. "You could lie down on the bench for a while."

"Tell a story," said Michael. "Tell about Rainbow and the wolf." So, after explaining to Stefan what had happened so far in the story, the man continued.

"When Waldo the wolf saw Rainbow the hen asleep in the hen house he grabbed her in his teeth and ran out across the chicken yard and down into the tunnel and under the fence and into the forest."

"Tell Steffy how sharp the wolf's teeth were," said Michael. "Sharp as *butcher* knives, Steffy."

"And not very clean," added Michael's father. "Wolves do not brush their teeth."

"I do," said Stefan.

"Go on, Daddy," said Michael.

"Well, as the wolf carried her from the hen house, Rainbow let out a loud frightened cackle. This woke up some of the other hens and *they* cackled."

"Did it wake up Mr. Tractorwheel?" said Michael.

"I don't know," said the man. "Did it?"

"Make it that it didn't," said Stefan.

"Right," said Michael.

So the man went on, saying, "Waldo carried Rainbow to his den, deep in the dark forest, and there he ate her and that is the end of the story. Now let's be quiet for a while."

"No!" shouted Michael and Stefan.

"He didn't eat her *yet!*" said Michael.

Stefan looked disappointed.

"O.K.," said the man. "He didn't eat her."

"Then tell some more, Daddy," said Michael.

"No, you boys are sleepy."

"We are not!" cried the boys.

"No?" said Michael's daddy. "Well, I am! If you'll be quiet for a few minutes I'll tell some more on the way home."

The boys closed their eyes and pretended to be asleep. In a moment there was the sound of snoring. Was Michael asleep? No. Stefan? No. *Michael's father was asleep!*

Chapter 4

WHEN Michael's father woke up, he took the two boys by the hand and they walked across the street to where the car was parked. Earlier the day had been cloudy, but now the sky was clear, or *almost* clear. There was just one cloud.

"Boys," said Michael's father, "I have what I think is a good idea. Let's put the top down."

"Yea!" cried the boys, and they all went to work unfastening fasteners and unzipping zippers and unsnapping snappers and tugging and pushing and lifting and grunting until finally the top was down and everyone was exhausted. Just then Michael felt something wet on his arm. A drop of water. He held out his hand. Another drop of water.

"Ohhh!" he moaned. "Daddy. It's raining!"

Sure enough. That one cloud had grown bigger and darker and was right over their heads, leaking raindrops.

"Boys," said Michael's father. "I have what I think is a good idea. Let's put the top *up!*"

"Ohhh!" moaned Michael. "I'm so tired." He lay down on his back on the sidewalk.

"Me too," said Stefan and lay down beside him.

Michael's father put the top up and then pressed his foot on the starter. It went r-r-r-r-r-r-r-r and the engine coughed but it didn't start. He pressed again. R-r-r-r-r, cough, cough. He pressed again. R-r-r-r, cough, cough.

"I smell gasoline," said Stefan.

"Me too," said Michael.

"She's flooded," said Michael's father.

They got out of the car and lifted the hood. Sure enough, the carburetor was so full of gasoline it was dripping.

"We'll have to sit and wait till it drains," he said.

"Tell some more about Rainbow," said Michael.

"What happened in the forest?" said Stefan.

They got back into the car and Michael's father went on with the story. "We left off where the wolf, Waldo, took the hen, Rainbow, to his den," said Michael's father. "Well, as soon as they reached his den the wolf said,

" 'Little hen, I am going to eat you.'

" 'Me?' said the hen.

" 'You.'

" 'Right now?' said the hen.

" 'As soon as I boil some water.'

" 'But I haven't had my breakfast,' said the hen.

" 'Now ain't that too bad,' said the Wolf.

" 'I will be fatter if I have breakfast,' said the hen. 'There will be more of me for you to eat.'

" 'Yeah? I never thought of that,' said the wolf. 'But you can't eat breakfast now.'

" 'Why not?'

" 'This is still the middle of the night. Breakfast is in the morning.'

" 'I'll just have to wait,' said the hen.

" '*You'll* have to wait?' said the wolf. 'What about *me?*'

" 'You'll have to wait too.'

" 'What are you trying to do, kid me?' said the wolf.

" 'A poor weak little hen like me, try to kid a great big handsome wolf like you?' said the hen. 'Don't be absurd.'

"The wolf turned his head and looked in a mirror. He was very vain, that wolf; loved to look at himself in the mirror, always putting stickum on his hair.

" 'What do you generally eat for breakfast?' said the wolf.

" 'Oh, a little grain, maybe.'

" 'I ain't got any grain,' said the wolf.

" 'Or worms.'

" 'And I ain't got any worms,' said the wolf. 'So it looks like I'll have to eat you the way you are, right now.'

" 'You have no grain or worms here in your den,' said Rainbow. 'But I wouldn't mind just scratching around outside your den while you boil the water and set the table.'

" 'Set *what* table?' said the wolf.

" 'I mean put out the knives and forks.'

" 'What knives and forks?!'

" 'I hope you weren't planning to eat me in your fingers,' said the hen.

" 'How do *you* eat chicken?' cried the wolf.

" 'I,' said the hen, 'do not eat chicken.'

"The wolf thought for a moment.

" 'How do I know you wouldn't run away if I let you scratch around outside?'

"The hen laughed. 'A poor little twerp of

a hen like me, try to run away from a ferocious intelligent superman of a wolf like you? Ha, ha, ha.'

"The wolf looked in the mirror again. He smoothed one eyebrow with a paw.

" 'I see what you mean,' he said. 'Well, go ahead. Eat up. Eat a lot. Get fat. I'll call you when breakfast is ready. I mean when *I'm* ready. And listen, Hen. Keep clucking so I can hear you. If you stop clucking I'll know that you are trying to escape. I'll come out and eat you right away.'

" 'Cluck, cluck,' said the hen.

" 'What did you say?' said the wolf.

" 'I said "cluck, cluck," ' said the hen.

" 'That's the idea,' said the wolf.

"So Rainbow the hen went clucking out into the clearing around the wolf's den, and the wolf went into his kitchen and turned on the gas range and put a big pot of water to boil. You realize, of course, that wolves do not have gas ranges and hens do not talk and this is all just a lot of nonsense."

"But go on," said Michael. "How does Rainbow get away?"

"*Does* Rainbow get away?" said Michael's father.

"And the wolf gets killed," said Stefan.

"How?" said Michael's father.

"Make it that the farmer has a little boy named Jimmy, and Jimmy kills the wolf," said Michael, "only not right away. Make it a longer story."

"All right," said Michael's father, "but let me start the car first and we can finish the story on the way home." He pressed the starter. This time the hood was up and the boys could see a stream of gasoline spurt right out of the carburetor.

"Boys, we're in trouble," said Michael's father.

"Goody, goody," said the boys.

"Goody my foot," said Michael's father. "I'll have to walk to a garage. Unless . . . maybe I can get that man over there to fix the carburetor." He pointed to a man who was bending over the engine of his own automobile, parked across the street.

The man did try to fix the carburetor but couldn't.

"I'll give you a shove in my car," said the man. "Maybe that'll start her."

So Michael and Stefan and Michael's father got in the car. The man drove his car around behind them and began to push. He pushed and he pushed, but still the engine wouldn't start. The man knew of a garage nearby. He phoned the garage and a truck came over and pushed the car into the garage and there a mechanic went to work on the carburetor. He took it apart.

"There's a hole in the float," he said.

"Can you fix it?" said Michael's father.

The man shook his head. "Have to put in a new one."

"How long will it take?"

"About an hour."

"Goody!" cried Michael. "You can tell about Rainbow for a whole hour."

"Oh, fine," said his father.

They went out and sat on the steps of a house next door to the garage, and the story was resumed.

Chapter 5

HE man sat in the middle of the step with his son Michael on one side and their good friend Stefan on the other. Michael was five and Stefan was six.

"Well," said Michael's father, "Rainbow the hen was in the forest outside the den of Waldo, the fiercest and most boring wolf in the world, when the sun came up and it was morning in the forest and on the farm. Mr. Tractorwheel and his boys got up and went out to do the chores before breakfast."

"What are chores?" said Stefan.

"Work. Little jobs of work. Milking the cows, feeding the pigs and chickens."

"Go on," said Michael.

"Young man, if you say 'go on' just once more, I'm going to have Rainbow pick up a club and go in the den and beat that wolf's brains out," said Michael's father.

"Yea, yea!" cried Stefan. "Do it!"

"No!" cried Michael. "Jimmy beats the wolf's brains out. You promised."

"All right, but stop saying 'Go on.' Well, Jimmy Tractorwheel was the farmer's youngest son. He was only about four or five, but strong, very strong. And clean. Always kept his hands and face clean. Ate very well, too, that Jimmy. Spinach, carrots, very little candy. And always slept late in the morning."

"On a *farm?*" said Michael.

"Well, he slept till somebody woke him up. Or if he was first to wake up he played very quietly in his room. Never disturbed his parents. Never went walking around the house in his bare feet either. Not in the winter time."

"Did Jimmy go to the hen house?" asked Michael.

"Yes, because it was his job to feed the chickens, and he came running to his father. 'Father, father, my pet hen Rainbow is gone!'

" 'Gone?'

" 'Come quickly!'

"So they ran to the hen house.

" 'Hmm,' said the farmer, 'she's gone all

right. Must have flown over the fence. She always was a wild one.'

" 'No, father,' said Jimmy. 'Look! See the big hole under the fence.'

" 'Sure enough,' said the farmer. 'She dug her way out.'

" 'No, father, I think the wolf dug a hole and carried Rainbow away.'

" 'What makes you think that?'

" 'Well, the hole is so big. Why would Rainbow dig such a *big* hole?'

"The farmer scratched his head, 'Mebbe you're right.'

" 'And look,' said Jimmy, 'a piece of wolf hair stuck here on the fence.'

" 'Danged if it ain't,' said the farmer. 'You win.'

"Mr. Tractorwheel and Jimmy went back to the house. The other boys were already at the breakfast table. Jimmy told them about Rainbow. They all shook their heads sadly except Tom, the fun-loving Tractorwheel, who was always making bum jokes.

" 'Did you see a pot of gold?' said Tom.

" 'No, why?' said Jimmy.

" 'They say there is always a pot of gold at the end of a Rainbow, and this sure looks like the end of Rainbow!'

"Tom slapped his leg and laughed so hard he fell over backward in his chair.

" 'I don't think it's funny,' said Jimmy.

" 'No, but it's true,' said his father. 'This is the end of Rainbow.'

" 'Maybe not,' said Jimmy. 'Maybe we could rescue Rainbow from the wolf.

" 'How?' said his father.

" 'The wolf lives in the forest,' said Jimmy. 'He must have taken Rainbow to his den.'

" 'And den what?' said Tom, falling over backward in his chair again.

" 'He ate her,' said the farmer.

" 'Maybe not,' said Jimmy. 'Maybe he's saving her for supper.'

" 'Could be,' said his father.

" 'I tell you what I suggest,' said Jimmy. 'Let's all go into the forest this morning and search.'

" 'Good idea,' said his father. 'You boys all do that. Wish I could join you, but I have to go to town to see a man about a well rope.'

" 'Swell idea, but I have a date to pitch horseshoes with Derwood Quigg,' said the oldest boy.

" 'I'm helping the Hargelroad girls make butter,' said the next oldest. 'They helped me last week.'

" 'And one good churn deserves another,'

cried Tom. 'As for me, I have to go to the
doctor to have some stitches taken in my
scalp.' The last time he had fallen over in his
chair he had hit his head on the base of the
stove, which is the sort of thing that happens

to people who go around making bum jokes.
  " 'I'll go alone,' said Jimmy.
  "And as soon as breakfast was over he took
a baseball bat and a small compass with a
luminous dial and genuine leather wrist strap
and entered the forest in search of his pet hen,
Rainbow."
  The garage men came to the door and
called to Michael's father.

"O.K.," he said. "She's O.K. now. I don't think she'll give you any more trouble."

Michael's father was very happy to get in the car and start home again.

"You boys have been *very good* today," he said as they drove through Central Park. "We've been gone from home almost eight hours and we haven't had any trouble at all. You deserve a reward. What will it be? Ice cream cones? Candy bars?"

"More!" cried the boys.

"More what?"

"More about Rainbow!"

"Next Sunday," said Michael's father. "In the meantime, please do not mention the name Rainbow to me again, or Waldo, or Jimmy Tractorwheel. Is that clear?"

The boys were so busy shooting at imaginary enemies coming out from behind trees and rocks that they did not stop to argue. They agreed to take ice cream cones as their reward. Double ice cream cones, that is.

Chapter 6

T BREAKFAST the following Sunday, Michael's father said, "Well, son, what about an excursion?"

"Yippee!" screamed Michael.

"What about my ear-drums?" said Michael's mother, holding her head.

"Washington Square?" said his father. Washington Square was a small park just a few blocks away.

"*That's* not an excursion!" said Michael. "Let's go to Jones Beach!"

"But it's too chilly to go swimming."

"We could play on the sand."

"I could fix you a lunch to take along," said Michael's mother.

"Do you realize how far it is to Jones Beach?" cried his father.

"Can we take Steffy?" cried Michael. "And fly a kite?"

"Oh, well, that's an idea," said his father, who liked to fly kites. "Maybe we could get that big box kite in the air." During the summer Michael's father had bought a box kite about as large as a kitchen stove and almost as heavy. In fact it was so heavy he had never been able to get it off the ground. He thought perhaps the wind at the beach would be strong enough to lift it—and then, of course, he wanted to go where his son wanted to go.

Michael went next door to get Stefan while his mother fixed a lunch for them and his father went to the basement to find the box kite, which was rolled up in a long paper bag.

And soon they were driving along the Franklin D. Roosevelt Drive toward the Triborough Bridge and the boys were firing imaginary fusillades at every ship in the East River. They crossed the bridge and passed LaGuardia Airport, where huge passenger planes were roaring in and out every few seconds, and then the boys settled down in the

front seat and Michael's father resumed the
story of Rainbow.

"Let's see, where were we?" he said. "Oh,
yes, Jimmy Tractorwheel went into the forest in search of Rainbow."

"He took a compass to find the wolf
with," said Michael.

"And a ball bat to hit him with," said
Stefan.

"No, the compass was to find his way
home," said Michael's father, "in case he got

lost. Anyway, Jimmy went bravely into the forest. He walked and he walked and he walked. Very quietly. He thought of calling Rainbow, but decided not to."

"The wolf might hear him," said Michael.

"And eat Rainbow," said Stefan.

"That's right. So he went quietly. And every few minutes he would stop and listen. He would turn his head slowly and listen very hard in every direction."

"Like this," said Michael. He turned his head slowly from side to side.

"Yes. Do you know what he was listening for?" said Michael's father.

"Clucking!" cried the boys.

"Yes. For a long time he heard nothing but the wind sighing in the pine trees and the birds chirping. And then, after a while, very faintly, far away, he heard it. 'Cluck, cluck, cluck, cluck. Cluck, cluck, cluck.' Rainbow! He turned his head this way and that way trying to decide where the clucking came from, and then he set off in what he thought was the right direction."

"As fast as his legs would carry him," said Michael.

"But quietly," said his father, "so as not to alarm the wolf. But to his great disappointment the clucking grew fainter instead of louder. Why was that?"

"Rainbow was getting tired?" said Stefan.

"No."

"The wolf took Rainbow in his den!" cried Michael.

"No. The clucking grew fainter because Jimmy was traveling in the wrong direction."

"Oh, yes," said the boys, snuggling harder against the front seat.

"So Jimmy Tractorwheel, instead of going so much *this* way, started going a little more *that* way, and the cluck-cluck-clucking grew louder and louder and louder. He was almost to the clearing. He took off his sneakers and walked in his stocking feet, on tiptoe; tip . . . toe . . . tip . . . toe. So-o-o-o quietly.

"Suddenly—*DING DONG, DING DONG!*—he heard a bell ringing. What could it be? He lay flat on his belly and peeked around a juniper bush and there in the clearing before him what did he see? Rainbow the hen—and across the clearing, in front of his den, stood the wolf, Waldo, wearing a dirty old pink apron."

"DING DONG, DING DONG!

"The wolf was ringing a big dinner bell.

" 'Come and get it,' cried the wolf. 'The water is boiling and I am very hungry. Hurry, hurry!'

"Rainbow did not move. Neither did Jimmy. He was waiting for Waldo to come closer so he could hit him with the baseball bat.

" 'Come on,' snarled the wolf. 'Get in here. Or must I come and drag you in?'

" 'I'm not quite finished with my breakfast.'

" 'Come on!'

" 'I'd like one more worm.'

" 'No!'

" 'One little bitsy *half* a worm?'

" 'NO!!' thundered the wolf.

" 'Please?'

"The wolf shook his head.

" 'Pretty please?'

" 'I am ready to eat you right now!' yelled the wolf. 'So come on!'

" 'Give me till you count to twenty-five,' said the hen.

" 'I will not! Quit stalling.'

" 'You don't know how to count to twenty-five,' said the hen.

" 'I certainly do,' said the wolf.

"And now," said Michael's father, "here we are. This is where we leave the car, and we walk through that underpass to the beach."

The boys could hear the roaring of the waves. They could taste the sea salt on their lips. They were so excited to be near the ocean that they forgot all about Rainbow and scampered off to the underpass, leaving Michael's father to carry a blanket, a lunch basket, two sweaters, a kite, and one, two, three, four, five, *six* balls of string.

Chapter 7

ICHAEL and Stefan took off their shoes and socks and ran in the deep soft white sand of Jones Beach, stumbling, falling, laughing, getting sand in their ears and hair and down their necks and up their sleeves and in their pockets. It was autumn, a cool day, and the water was too chilly to swim in, but the boys raced along the damp sand at the water's edge, and once in a while a wave would come up farther than the others and lick their heels with an icy tongue.

Meanwhile Michael's father was sitting on a blanket assembling the big box kite. There were so many sticks to be fitted into so many other sticks. Michael's father had his glasses on and seemed to be working hard. Presently he stood up and called to the boys.

The kite was ready. It was as large as Michael.

"Now watch her fly," said Michael's father. He ran across the beach, holding the kite by its string. It just bumped along on the sand.

"Let me try it," said Michael. He could hardly pull the big kite, but he ran across the beach with it. Still it wouldn't fly. Then Stefan ran with it and *still* it wouldn't fly.

"The wind blows it down instead of up," said Michael's father.

"Must be something wrong," said Michael.

His father nodded.

"You can fix it, Daddy," said Michael. "With courage and patience you can fix anything. Come on, Steffy. Let's be cowboys." And the boys galloped away.

Michael's father studied the box kite very carefully and then he untied a string here and put it there, and untied a string there and put it here. The boys raced by on imaginary broncos, firing imaginary pistols into the real air. Michael's father called to them.

"I'm going to try once more," he said. "I am going to run from here to the edge of the water. If she doesn't go up in the air by the time I get to the water, I am going to throw her in the ocean."

"Yipe!" cried the boys. They didn't know which would be more fun, to see the kite in the sky or in the ocean.

Michael's father held the kite high in one hand. In the other hand he held a ball of string. He began to run. Suddenly the kite left his hand. It began to climb. Slowly but steadily . . . up, up, up. Michael's father was running hard, the boys were shouting. Michael's father, looking up at the kite, tripped over a piece of driftwood and fell on his face in the sand, but he held onto the string.

Higher and higher went the kite. Michael's father let the boys take turns holding the string. It was exciting because if you accidentally let the string go, the kite would come tumbling down out of the sky.

When lunchtime came they hauled the kite in and sat on the blanket and opened the basket. There were sandwiches and tomatoes and a thermos of milk and some oranges and cookies. The boys ate as much as they wanted, and then stretched out on the blanket in the warm sun.

"Think you could take a snooze?" said Michael's father.

The boys said no.

"I could," said Michael's father.

"First some Rainbow," said Michael.

"Will that make you sleepy?"

The boys said no.

"It will me!" said Michael's father. "Well, where were we? Oh yes. Almost finished. The wolf said Rainbow had to come in this very minute and be eaten.

" 'If you want to eat me,' shouted the proud little hen, 'you'll have to catch me first.' And, turning, she scurried across the clearing toward the bush where Jimmy lay hiding.

" 'Ha, ha,' cried the wolf. 'I can catch you in two leaps.' He squatted on his haunches with his big butcher-knife teeth glistening in the morning sunlight and made one great leap that carried him to the center of the clearing. And at that moment, five-year-old James Tractorwheel jumped out from behind the juniper bush, holding the baseball bat firmly in both hands.

" 'Halt!' said Jimmy.

" 'Jimmy!' cried the hen.

" 'YIPE!' screamed the wolf.

"Rainbow was so overjoyed to see Jimmy that she flapped her wings and flew right to his shoulder and perched there.

"Jimmy put all of his muscle and all of his weight into one swing of the Louisville Slugger and brought it down on the wolf's head. BONG! The wolf smiled foolishly and sank to his knees. Now what I want to know is this. Do you boys want Jimmy to hit the wolf again and kill him, or tie him up with some rope and drag him home and put him in a cage, or what? How do you want the story to end? Steffy, you're company. You say first."

Stefan smiled shyly and shrugged his shoulders.

"Ask Mike," he said. "It's his story."

"Steffy, you are a very good, kind, polite boy, a credit to your mother and father," said Michael's father. Then he turned to his son and said, "Michael, you are also a very good, kind, polite boy, and, as Steffy says, it is your story. What shall we do with the wolf?"

"Make it that he gets up and runs away," said Michael.

His father could hardly believe his ears.

"Let the wolf run away?"

"Yes," said Michael. "As fast as his legs will carry him."

"You don't want him killed? Or even captured?"

Michael shook his head, no.

"This is the first time you've ever wanted a wolf to get away. What is this, be-kind-to-wolves week?"

Michael's eyes were shining and he spoke in a loud whisper. "If the wolf gets

away he will come back and steal Rainbow again!"

"Yea!" cried Stefan.

"*You want that to happen?*" cried Michael's father.

Michael nodded his head, yes.

"Say! Whose side are you on, anyway?" said his father.

"You can kill the wolf at the very end, but

this way we can have more story!" said Michael.

"Yea!" said Stefan.

"So go on," said Michael.

And so Michael's father made it that the wolf got up from his knees and staggered into the deep green forest and then the boys took a good rest on the blanket on the sand with the waves roaring agreeably in their ears.

Chapter 8

MICHAEL and Stefan were lying on a blanket on the beach. Between them lay Michael's father. It was the boys' naptime, but, as usual, only Michael's father was asleep.

The boys were lying with their eyes closed listening to the noise of the ocean: a soft *ssswhishhh* followed by a loud *RRROARRR! Sssswishhh . . . RRROARRR!*

The *ssswhishhh* was made by weary old waves as they slipped out to sea after trying to climb clear up the beach and onto the blanket with Michael and Stefan. As each thin old wave slid down the sandy slope away from the beach it ran smack into a fat new wave coming *toward* the beach. The fat new wave would trip over the thin old wave, trip and stumble and tumble and flop right on

its face with an angry *RRROARRR.*
Ssswishhh . . . RROARRR! Ssswishhh
. . . RRROARR!

Right beside the two boys, Michael's father was making a similar noise, going *aahhhh . . . pooooooo! . . . aahhh . . . poooooo!* Sometimes the noises would get mixed up and go *Ssswishhh . . . aahhh; RRROARRR . . . pooooo.* Or even *RRROARRR . . . aahhh; ssswishhh . . . pooooo.*

It would have put the boys to sleep if it had not been naptime.

Michael opened his eyes. He yawned. He scratched his knee where a fly had been sitting. He rubbed one eye and rubbed his nose and yawned again. "Ooooooh," he yawned. Then he rolled over on his side and propped himself up on one elbow.

"Steffy," he whispered.

Stefan opened one eye and whispered, "What?"

"You asleep?" said Michael.

Stefan opened the other eye, thought for a moment and said, "No."

"Let's play a game," whispered Michael.

"Your father said to be quiet till rest is over," whispered Stefan.

"But my father is asleep!" whispered Michael.

"I am not," said his father, opening his eyes.

"Daddy! You were!" cried Michael.

"But I'm not now!"

"Good!" said Michael. "Then you can play a game too."

"Oh, fine," said Michael's father.

"Goody, goody!" cried the boys.

"You were quiet while I took my nap. I'll play a game with you. What shall we play? Tag? Hide-and-seek . . ."

"Bunnies and the wolf!" cried both boys, dancing happily in the sand.

"Bunnies and the what?" said Michael's father.

"The wolf!" cried the two boys.

Michael's father shut his eyes.

"Please, please, please," said Michael, crawling on top of his father. "The blanket will be your house and you will try to capture

the bunnies and put them in prison in your
house and eat them, only they get away. You
leave the door unlocked a little."

"Get your sandy foot out of my mouth,"
said Michael's father.

"Look out, he's a wolf," cried Stefan—
and pulled Michael away.

"I am not," said Michael's father. "Anything else. Not a wolf."

Soon they were playing bunnies and the
fox. The bunnies, Michael and Stefan, would
dance around the blanket singing, "ya, ya,
ya, you can't catch me," until suddenly the
fox, Michael's father, would reach out and
grab a bunny and drag him into the house and
put him in the icebox, but as soon as the fox
turned his back the bunny would escape,
shouting, "Ya, ya, ya, you left the door unlocked!" After the bunnies had been caught
about twenty times, Michael's father said,
"Well, boys, we'd better start home now."

"No!" cried Michael. "Not so soon!"

Stefan didn't say anything, but he looked
very unhappy.

"You have been such good boys we can

get ice cream or popcorn to eat on the way home," said Michael's father.

"Yea!" cried the boys, forgetting how much they hated to leave the beach and thinking only of ice cream and popcorn.

As they drove home, Michael's father picked up the story where Waldo the wolf ran into the forest.

"Jimmy Tractorwheel carried Rainbow the hen all the way home on his shoulder," said Michael's father, "and when they arrived at the Tractorwheel farm, Jimmy's mother and father and brothers were in the yard, and they all cheered 'Hurrah, hurrah,' and shouted, 'Good boy, Jimmy!' and 'Welcome home, Rainbow.'

"Jimmy wanted to tell his brothers that he would rather have had their help in finding Rainbow than all this cheering afterward, but he said nothing. Jimmy loved his brothers and when you love people you do not go around finding fault with them. Or at least you shouldn't.

" 'We have filled up that hole the wolf dug under the fence,' said the farmer, Jimmy's father, 'so Rainbow will be safe in the chicken yard.'

" 'What did you fill it with?' asked Jimmy.

" 'Dirt.'

" 'But if the wolf came again he could dig a tunnel in the dirt the same as he did before,' said Jimmy.

" 'That's true,' said the farmer. 'Yep. I never thought of that. What do you suggest, Jimmy?'

" 'I suggest that we dig a deep trench underneath the fence all the way around the chicken yard and fill it with concrete,' said Jimmy. 'Then we will cover it with dirt, and if a wolf tries to dig his way under the fence he will run into the concrete.'

" 'Say, that's a good idea,' said the farmer. 'No wolf can dig through a concrete wall.'

" 'Not only that,' said Jimmy, 'but if he tries, he will stub his toenails and maybe he will yell *Ouch* and we will hear him and come running out of the house and take care of Mr. Wolf.'

" 'Good idea,' said the farmer, and all of Jimmy's brothers agreed that it was a good idea, but when it came to digging the trench that afternoon they were all busy somewhere else and Jimmy had to do it by himself. He didn't mind, though. He knew it would strengthen his shoulder muscles for swimming and canoe-paddling.

"When the trench was dug he lined it with boards and poured in concrete. Next day when the concrete was very, very hard, Jimmy attached the bottom of the chicken yard fence to some hooks he had put in the concrete, and covered the concrete with dirt. The chicken yard now looked exactly as it had looked when Waldo the wolf came the first time, but it was certainly not the same,

and if Waldo tried to dig into the chicken yard again, oh, brother, what a surprise he would get."

Michael's father paused here to eat a handful of Michael's popcorn. He also ate one of the fruit drops that Stefan carried. Stefan had a slight cough and carried fruit drops to suck when his throat began to tickle. The boys could hardly wait to hear what happened when Waldo came to the chicken yard again. Of course they knew perfectly well he *would* come again.

"Make it that he comes again that *very night!*"

"First, I'd better make it that we get some gasoline," said his father.

He drove into a filling station and the boys sat quietly eating popcorn while the filling-station man put in gasoline, checked the oil and washed the windshield.

Chapter 9

AS THEY pulled out of the filling station Michael said, "Go on, Daddy. Make it that Waldo comes to steal Rainbow again that very night. Oh, Steffy, isn't this scary?"

"I don't want to make it too scary," said Michael's father.

"Yes!" cried the boys. "Make it *too* scary! Horribly, horribly scary."

"Time out," said Michael's father. "My voice is tired."

"Here," said Stefan, and handed him a fruit drop.

"Well," said Michael's father when he had finished the fruit drop, "Waldo ran off into the forest, remember?" The boys nodded their heads, and Michael's father continued.

"Waldo was very angry. 'Who does that little Jimmy Tractorwheel think he is, anyway?' the wolf said to himself. 'Hitting me with a ball bat. And him only five years old.'

"Waldo was so angry he swore he would get even with Jimmy Tractorwheel. He would steal Rainbow the hen again and this time he would eat her at once, so that Jimmy could not save her. 'I will do it tomorrow night,' the wolf said to himself. 'I would do it tonight only I have such a headache from being hit with the ball bat.' It is a good thing he decided to wait, because that gave Jimmy's concrete wall time to get hard.

"The next night was as dark as the inside of a black velvet pocketbook. No moon. No stars. The only light came from the tiny flashes of fireflies. 'What a perfect night to steal a hen,' said the wolf to himself as he came out of his den at midnight. 'Boy, is it dark!' he said. Just then he bumped into a tree. 'A little too dark,' he said. 'I bruised my nose!'

"He went back into his den and got a glass fruit jar. He caught a lot of fireflies and put them in the fruit jar. When they all flashed at once he could see pretty well, and so he arrived at the farm without bumping into any more trees.

" 'Ah! Perfect!' he said to himself as he

looked around the farmyard. 'Not a Tractor-wheel in sight. Everybody in bed, including that little smarty-pants Jimmy. Will he be surprised when he comes out in the morning and finds another hole under his chicken yard fence and his pet hen Rainbow missing! I guess I'll eat her right in the chicken yard and leave some of the feathers, so he'll *know* I ate her. Heh, heh, heh.'

"Waldo crept toward the chicken yard. He held the jar of fireflies under his topcoat and let out just enough light to show him where he had dug a hole under the fence. It was filled up—but with very soft earth.

" 'This is too easy,' he said to himself. 'This is like stealing candy from a baby. In fact that Jimmy Tractorwheel is hardly more than a baby. Imagine him, a mere five-year-old boy, hitting me, *Waldo the wolf*, with a ball bat!'

"The memory of that sock on the head made Waldo so angry that he stripped off his topcoat, put the jar of fireflies on the ground and began to dig furiously. The soft earth was easy digging. His sharp toenails ripped it up and threw it back between his front legs, and it rattled against his empty belly, sounding like a drum and reminding him that he was mighty hungry. He had his nose right in the earth. And then all of a sudden his toenails hit the concrete wall. He was digging so fast that his nose banged against the rough concrete.

" 'OUCH!' he yelped. 'I skinned my nose!'

"In the farmhouse, Jimmy Tractorwheel rolled over in his bed, but he did not quite wake up.

"Waldo brought his firefly flashlight over to see what he had bumped into. 'Aha,' he snarled. 'They put a rock in the hole. Thought they'd fool old Waldo that way. Heh, heh. I'll show 'em. I'll dig *around* the rock!' He didn't realize that he was up against a concrete wall.

"He put down his light and began a new hole right next to the old one. Faster and faster he dug. The earth shot out and rattled against his empty belly. *Ratta-tat-tat-tat, ratta-tat-tat-tat*, like a drum. And then, again—

" 'OUCH!' he yelped. 'I skinned my nose!' This time his yelp was a little louder, or maybe Jimmy was not quite so deep in sleep, but anyway Jimmy woke up. He sat up in bed.

" 'Did I hear something?' Jimmy said to himself. He listened for a minute. 'Guess not,' he said, and lay down again.

"Meanwhile Waldo was angrily snarling to himself, 'Another rock! I'll show 'em, I'll go clear around to the other side of the chicken yard and dig there. I guess they wouldn't think of putting a rock over there.'

"He picked up his fireflies and his topcoat and slunk around to the opposite side of the chicken yard. And again he began to dig. Faster and faster flew the soft black earth. 'Won't be long now,' panted Waldo. And then—

" 'OUCH! I skinned my nose!'

"This time Jimmy Tractorwheel was not asleep. He distinctly heard a sound. It was so far away he could not tell what it was, but he went to his window and looked out. He could see nothing but an occasional glow of light as if from an unusually large firefly. It came from the direction of the chicken yard.

" 'That's funny,' said Jimmy to himself. 'Must be an unusually large firefly!' He decided to put on his bathrobe and slippers and stay at the window for a little while just to watch and listen."

"And now, boys," said Michael's father, "I hate to interrupt the story but here we are at the Triborough Bridge and I have to get a quarter out of my pocket to pay the toll with."

"Let me hand it to the policeman," said Michael.

"You did it last time," said Stefan. "Let me."

"O.K., Steffy, you do it."

So when the car stopped at the toll gate it was Stefan who handed the quarter to the policeman.

"Thanks, sonny," said the policeman, and off went the car across the big bridge.

Chapter 10

W E'RE almost at the end of the story and I'll try to finish it before we get home," said Michael's father as they drove down the Franklin D. Roosevelt Drive.

"Make it that Waldo skins his nose again," said Michael.

"Oh, no," said his father. "Waldo has skinned his nose three times already."

"But it's so funny," said Stefan. The very thought of Waldo skinning his nose made the boys laugh so hard they almost fell out of the car.

"But this time," said Michael's father, "the wolf decided to try to dig sideways. So he found a fresh spot in the earth beside the chicken yard and began digging with his left front paw and his left rear paw, so in case he ran into another rock he would not skin his nose. The earth was soft and Waldo was digging fast when all of a sudden,

" 'OUCH!" he yelped. 'I skinned my side!' "

Michael's father had to stop the story for a few moments because the boys were laughing so hard. Then he continued:

"This time Jimmy Tractorwheel heard the wolf quite clearly. He left the window and ran into his father's room.

" 'Papa, Papa,' cried Jimmy.

"Farmer Tractorwheel woke up with a snort. 'Jimmy!' he said. 'What's the matter? Have a nightmare?' Children of Jimmy's age often do have nightmares.

" 'No, no. The wolf is trying to get in the chicken yard again!' cried Jimmy.

" 'Now you go back to bed,' said his father. 'You'll be all right.'

" 'I heard him!' said Jimmy.

" 'And don't run around the house in your bare feet,' said his father.

" 'I've got my slippers on,' said Jimmy.

"Down in the yard, Waldo the wolf had given up digging sideways and was trying to dig backwards, with his hind feet. He was digging along all right when suddenly he let out the biggest yelp of all.

" 'OUCH! I skinned my behind!'

"The yelp could be heard clearly in Jimmy's father's bedroom.

" 'There!' said Jimmy.

" 'YIPE!' cried his father, jumping out of bed. 'You're right, Jimmy. It *is* the wolf. We'll catch him.' They raced through the house waking up Jimmy's brothers. Jimmy's father took a shotgun, Jimmy took his Louisville Slugger and the other boys took ropes and old tennis rackets. Quietly they crept down the stairs and out of the house.

" 'We'll surround him,' whispered Jimmy's father. 'O.K., Jimmy?'

" 'O.K., Papa,' whispered Jimmy. 'We can tell where he is by the flashing of that light.'

"Half of them crept to one side of the chicken house and the others to the other side. Waldo did not hear them he was so furious. He kept digging, digging, digging. First frontwards, and he would yelp, 'Ouch, I skinned my nose!' Then sideways: 'Ouch, I skinned my side.' Then backwards, 'Ouch, I skinned my behind!'

"Suddenly Farmer Tractorwheel switched on a big flashlight. It lighted up the whole chicken yard. Waldo the wolf turned toward the light, snarling viciously.

" 'Stay where you are or I'll shoot,' said Farmer Tractorwheel.

" 'I am trapped!' cried the wolf.

" 'You are!' cried all the Tractorwheels.

"Then the ferocious wolf began to whine and cry. 'Oh, please do not hurt me,' he whined. 'I meant no harm. I only wanted to play with the pretty hen. She is my friend.'

"Farmer Tractorwheel said, 'Jimmy, it was your good work that caused the wolf to be caught. You can decide what to do with him. Shall I shoot him?'

" 'Just a minute, Papa,' said Jimmy. 'May I ask the wolf a few questions?'

" 'Your witness,' said the farmer.

" 'Wolf,' said Jimmy. 'What makes you so mean?'

" 'Me?' said the wolf. 'I ain't mean.'

" 'You would eat my chicken,' said Jimmy.

" 'Didn't you ever eat no chicken?' said the wolf.

" 'Well, yes,' said Jimmy. 'But we raise chickens and take care of them. You only steal and eat them. If you had your way you would kill off all the chickens and there wouldn't be any more. But we keep having more all the time. You're destructive.'

" 'I see what you mean,' said the wolf. 'But I ain't never had a chance to be a farmer boy. I never been nothing but a wolf all my life. I never had no opportunities. I ain't even been to school.'

" 'Don't say *ain't*,' said Jimmy. 'There's no such word.'

" 'There ain't?' said the wolf.

" 'Oh, shoot him,' said Tom Tractorwheel. 'I want to get back to bed.'

"Papa Tractorwheel raised the shotgun to his shoulder.

" 'Wait,' said Jimmy. 'There is something in what the wolf says.'

" 'Don't be a softie,' said Tom. 'Kill that wolf or he will keep coming back and stealing chickens.'

" 'Tom's right,' said Papa Tractorwheel.

" 'No, no,' cried the wolf. 'Never again.'

" 'But if we kill this wolf there will still be plenty of other wolves to come and steal our chickens,' said Jimmy.

" 'That's true,' said Papa Tractorwheel. 'What's one wolf less?'

" 'One wolf less is one wolf less,' said Tom, 'and I'm colder than a well-digger's toe.'

"It was really chilly there in the farmyard in the middle of the night with nothing on but pajamas and bathrobes and slippers.

" 'What do you say, Jimmy?' said Papa Tractorwheel. 'We can't stand here all night arguing.'

" 'I think we ought to lock the wolf up in a cage,' said Jimmy. 'Tomorrow I will

come and talk to him. I will try to learn about wolves so I can work out a plan for solving the wolf problem.'

"So Waldo was locked up and every day Jimmy would come and ask him questions about how a wolf is treated by his parents and what makes him so fierce. The more Waldo talked about his fierceness the gentler he grew, until finally he was allowed out of the cage on a leash. Jimmy and Waldo wrote a book about wolves which was read by the farmers and the wolves in that part of the country and helped them to understand each other. They all became quite friendly and some wolves even worked on the farms, as sheepdogs. And all because Jimmy Tractorwheel was brave and kind and *very curious.*

"And that," said Michael's father, "is the end of the story."

"No!" cried Michael. "Waldo gets away one dark night and creeps to the hen house . . ."

"I said that was the end of the story."

"But we aren't quite home yet!"

"Michael!" said his father.

The two boys were silent for a while and then Michael said, "Could Waldo be a sheepdog?"

"Sure," said Stefan.

"With such big teeth?" said Michael.

"Probably wore a muzzle," said Stefan.

"Start it all over again," said Michael.

"Yes!" said Stefan.

"You boys have been so very good today," said Michael's father, "I will take you on another excursion next Sunday."

"And tell it again," said Stefan.

"Yea!" cried Mike.

And so it was that when Michael and Stefan got on the elevated train the following Sunday with Michael's father, the people directly behind them heard these words:

"Once upon a time there was a hen named Rainbow."

A NOTE ON THE TYPE USED

This book has been set in a Linotype adaptation of a type designed by William Caslon, the first (1692–1766), greatest of English letter founders. The Caslon face, an artistic, easily read type, has had two centuries of ever increasing popularity in our own country—it is of interest to note that the first copies of the Declaration of Independence and the first paper currency distributed to the citizens of the newborn nation were printed in this type face.

This reissue of Wolf Story was printed by Cushing-Malloy, Inc., Ann Arbor, Michigan and bound by John H. Dekker and Sons, Grand Rapids, Michigan.

Typography and binding design by Warren Chappell.